T0197579

THE MAGIC

IN THE WORLD

Dr. Fariba P. Ansari

To order additional copies of this book, contact:
Xlibris
844-714-8691
www.Xlibris.com
Orders@Xlibris.com

ISBN: Softcover   978-1-6698-4551-5
        EBook   978-1-6698-4550-8

Print information available on the last page

Rev. date: 09/12/2022

DEDICATION

TO MY BEAUTIFUL CHILDREN ARMAN & ANITA,
MY NEPHEWS MATHEW & ARTIN WHO BRING SO
MUCH LOVE & JOY TO MY LIFE & TO BEAUTIFUL
CHILDREN ALL OVER THE WORLD.

I OFFER THIS BOOK TO ALL OF YOU WITH
LOVE AND PEACE IN MY HEART.

ACKNOWLEDGMENT

THE MEMORY OF MY BELOVED FATHER AND MY
LOVING MOTHER WHO ALWAYS INSPIRED ME
TO LEARN AND EXTEND MY KNOWLEDGE

IN ADDITION, THE MEMORY OF MY BELOVED TEACHER,
MS. MOMENI IN HIGH SCHOOL, WHO ALWAYS
ENCOURAGED ME TO BE AN AUTHOR &
HER KIND WORDS STAYED WITH ME.

TO ALL THE TEACHERS OF GREAT TRUTH AND TO THE
ILLUSTRATORS & TO ALL THE PUBLICATION STAFF.

FROM THE BEGINNING (ALPHA) TO THE END
(OMEGA) TO THE SOURCE OF ALL INSPIRATION
DIVINE WITH MUCH LOVE AND GRATITUDE.

ON A WARM, SUNNY AND BEAUTIFUL EARLY DAY IN SPRING.

LITTLE LILY WOKE UP FROM A LONG SLEEP.
AS SHE LOOKED OUTSIDE THE WINDOW,
SUDDENLY SHE SAW DARK CLOUDS COMING TOGETHER.

THE WIND STARTED HOWLING AND SHAKING THE DOORS.
SHE HEARD THE SOUND OF THE WINDOWS RATTLING.
AND CRACKLING WITH EACH GUST OF THE HOWLING WIND.

SHE BECAME SCARED AND CRIED,
"OH NO WHAT WAS THAT?"

SHE SIGHED TO HERSELF
"I THINK IT'S BETTER IF I JUST CLOSE ALL MY WINDOWS
AND LOCK ALL MY DOORS. I WILL CRAWL UNDER MY
WARM COZY BLANKET AND STAY IN BED ALL DAY.

HER FRIEND SARAH WHO WAS IN ANOTHER ROOM
HEARD LILY AND HOW SCARED SHE WAS.
SHE WALKED OVER TO LILY'S ROOM AND WHISPERED
"LILY, HOLD MY HAND. COME WITH ME TO MY
ROOM AND LOOK AT THE BEAUTIFUL TREES."

AS SOON AS THEY GOT TO THE SARAH'S ROOM, LILY
JUMPED TO THE WINDOW AND LOOKED OUTSIDE.

SHE WAS AMAZED BY THE VIEW.

LILY OPENED THE WINDOW AND POKED HER HEAD
OUTSIDE. SHE TOOK A DEEP BREATH AND COULD
SMELL THE DELICIOUS FRAGRANCE OF THE FLOWERS,
WHICH WAS FLOATING THROUGH THE AIR.

11

"OH MY!!! LOOK AT THE BEAUTIFUL BUTTERFLIES. THEY ARE PRETTY!! THE TREES ARE AMAZING AND THE FLOWERS SMELL SO SWEET!" LILY SHRIEKED WITH JOY.

"I AM READY TO GO OUT AND PLAY."

SARAH SAID "YES, THE CLOUDS CLEARED UP AND IT'S A BEAUTIFUL DAY. LET'S GO OUT AND START THE DAY."

THEY WERE PLAYING AND LAUGHING. THEY STARTED
CHASING THE BUTTERFLIES, THROUGH THE LUSCIOUS
GREEN GRASS AND BEAUTIFUL FLOWERS. THE
BUTTERFLIES LEAD THEM TO THE RIVER. THEY SAW
A BIG, BUMPY LOG FLOATING IN THE RIVER.

THEY JUMPED ON IT AND ENDED UP IN
A BEAUTIFUL CLEAR BLUE LAKE.

THE WATER WAS SO CLEAR THAT THEY COULD
SEE THE FISH SWIMMING BELOW THEM.

SHE SAW THE MOST BEAUTIFUL GREEN TREES
SHE HAD EVER SEEN. THE SUN WAS PEEKING
THROUGH THE LUSCIOUS BRANCHES.

SHE SAW ORBS AROUND THE TREES, DANCING AROUND
MAKING THE LEAVES SO GREEN, SHINY, AND BRIGHT.

SHE SAW TWO MAJESTIC BUTTERFLIES, CHASING
EACH OTHER THROUGH THE BEAUTIFUL BLOSSOMS.

THEY HAD SO MUCH FUN, THAT THEY LOST
TRACK OF TIME. THE SUN WAS SETTING AND IT
WAS ASTONISHING. THEY HAD NEVER SEEN A
SUNSET SO BEAUTIFUL AND MAGNIFICENT.

IT WAS SUCH A MEMORABLE DAY, THEY WISHED IT
WOULD NEVER END BUT THEY WERE HAPPY AND
THANKFUL THAT THEY HAD SUCH A GREAT TIME.

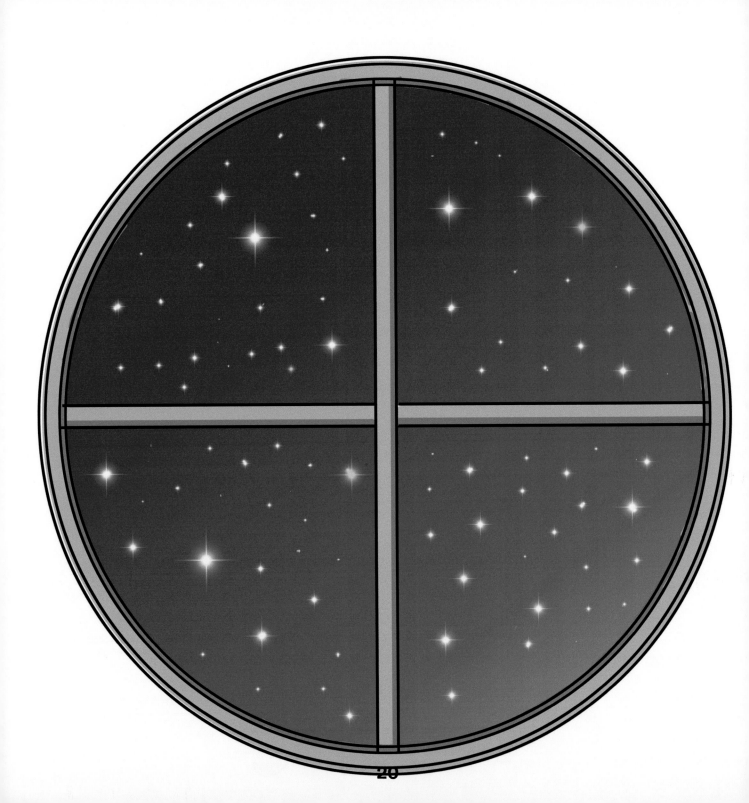

AS THEY ENTERED INSIDE THE HOUSE, LILY LOOKED
OUT THE WINDOW AND STARED AT THE SKY.
AGAIN, SHE SIGHED "OH MY, THE SUN IS
SETTING AND IT IS GETTING SO DARK."
AS SOON AS SHE SAID THAT SARAH GENTLY TOLD HER
"LILY, LOOK RIGHT THERE. LOOK OUT THE WINDOW."
SARAH POINTED TO A WINDOW ABOVE THEM.

LOOK AT THE BEAUTIFUL SKY. THE STARS
ARE SPARKLING AND SO BRIGHT.

LILY LOOKED AT THE WINDOW ABOVE ON THE CEILING.

SHE WAS AMAZED AT HOW MANY STARS SHE COULD
SEE IN THE SKY. SOME OF THE STARS WERE BRIGHT
AND SOME TWINKLED AND DANCED IN THE DARK SKY.

LILY STARTED SMILING AND SAID, "IT'S A BEAUTIFUL SKY
WITH ALL THE SPARKLING STARS. I THINK I AM READY TO
HAVE A GOOD NIGHTS SLEEP. SWEET DREAMS SARAH".

"SWEET DREAMS LILY"

Printed in the United States
by Baker & Taylor Publisher Services